Eddie
Harold's Little Brother

By **Ed Koch** and **Pat Koch Thaler**

Illustrated by **James Warhola**

G. P. PUTNAM'S SONS   NEW YORK

G. P. Putnam's Sons, a division of Penguin Young Readers Group,

345 Hudson Street, New York, NY 10014.

G. P. Putnam's Sons, Reg. U.S. Pat. & Tm. Off.

Published simultaneously in Canada. Manufactured in China by South China Printing Co. Ltd.

Designed by Cecilia Yung and Gina DiMassi. Text set in Else Semibold.

The art was done in watercolor on Arches paper.

Library of Congress Cataloging-in-Publication Data

Koch, Ed, 1924–

Eddie : Harold's little brother / by Ed Koch and Pat Koch Thaler ;

illustrated by James Warhola.   p. cm.   Summary: Eddie wants to be like his big brother,

a very good athlete, but is not good at sports, so Harold helps him discover how to use his own

special talent—talking. [1. Brothers—Fiction. 2. Sports—Fiction. 3. Public speaking—Fiction.

4. Individuality—Fiction. 5. Koch, Ed, 1924– —Childhood and youth—Fiction.]

I. Thaler, Pat Koch. II. Warhola, James, ill. III. Title. PZ7.K7885Ed 2004 [Fic]—dc22 2003025138

ISBN 0-399-24210-4

1 3 5 7 9 10 8 6 4 2

First Impression

Special thanks to our editor,
Nancy Paulsen,
a creative and supportive collaborator.
—Ed Koch, Pat Koch Thaler,
and James Warhola

For Harold and all the champions in our family:
Kayla, Jordan, Noah, Hannah, Sasha, Perri and Benjamin
—*Ed Koch and Pat Koch Thaler*

For Mary and Oonagh
—*James Warhola*

Eddie and Harold were brothers. Harold, who was older, was a terrific athlete. He hit home runs in baseball and scored touchdowns in football. Playing basketball, he made the ball swoosh through the basket. When Harold played, he got cheers. All the kids wanted Harold on their team.

Eddie wanted to be like Harold. It was baseball season, so he asked
Harold to practice with him. Harold threw balls and Eddie tried to catch
them. But the harder Eddie tried, the more he messed up. Some days, Eddie
managed to catch the ball and then he'd grin and ask, "How am I doing, Harold?"

"Better, Eddie. But you need a lot more practice."

Eddie was even worse at the games. When he played in the outfield and missed a ball coming right to him, kids on his team groaned.

"Eddie, are you playing for the other team or for us?" said one, throwing his cap on the ground.

Harold didn't say anything, but Eddie knew he was disappointed.

At first, Harold stood by his little brother. "If you want me, you have to let Eddie play too."

All the team members complained and made faces, but they always ended up letting Eddie play.

One Saturday morning, Eddie woke up to find Harold gone. This was strange because Harold always woke Eddie in time for the regular Saturday game.

Eddie dressed quickly, grabbed his baseball mitt, and hurried off to the ball field. Harold was just stepping up to home plate.

"Harold!" Eddie called.

Harold turned. He didn't look at all pleased to see his younger brother.

"What do you want?"

"Hey, Harold!" the pitcher yelled. "Stop wasting time! We're playing a game!"

"What about me?" Eddie protested. "I want to play too!"

"Not now," Harold shouted to Eddie. He turned to the pitcher and raised his bat. "I'm ready."

Eddie punched his fist into his mitt. Why was Harold being so mean?

Eddie was sad thinking that Harold was ashamed of him, but it didn't keep him from being proud of his big brother. Eddie was always telling everyone he knew what a terrific athlete Harold was. Nothing made Eddie happier than to talk—especially about his big brother.

Eddie sat out the game on the bench. But still, he cheered for his team. He was disappointed that they hadn't let him play, but he loved watching Harold and the other guys.

After the game Harold and the others came off the field and sat around on the grass. Eddie ran over. "Did you see that pop fly their first baseman missed?" he asked. "And what a great double play in the second inning."

Eddie remembered everything that had happened during the game, even the tiniest detail, like how everyone started laughing when the other team's third baseman started sneezing and missed an easy grounder. The kids listened eagerly as Eddie covered the highlights of the game.

"I thought you guys would lose until Harold hit a homer with bases loaded in the fourth inning. And that double play later in the game was fantastic. And did you guys notice how those big clouds in the sky look like different animals? Look—there's one that's like an elephant with its trunk raised," he continued.

As he pointed at a cloud on the horizon, Eddie noticed that the boys were losing interest. Soon Harold and Eddie headed home.

The next Saturday was beautiful and sunny. Eddie got up early to make sure he'd be included. When Harold and Eddie got to the field, the other guys were practicing.

"Okay, Eddie. We're counting on you to do better today," the second baseman said. "And don't forget, we want you to give us the play-by-play after the game."

The other team arrived and the game started. In the second inning, with the bases loaded, it was Eddie's turn at bat. He clutched the bat and concentrated hard on the pitcher, waiting for the ball. He would hit that ball so hard, it would disappear into the clouds! Then he would run around the bases and arrive back at home plate with the others cheering, and Harold roaring his approval, and—

"Strike one!" called the umpire. The ball had flown right past Eddie's bat.

"Come on, Eddie! We need a hit!"

Eddie squinted hard at the pitcher and then—

"Strike two!

"Strike three! You're out!"

Instead of cheers, there were boos. Eddie walked off the field, embarrassed. He couldn't bear to meet Harold's eye.

But then Harold rescued the game. He clobbered the ball, which soared right over the outstretched arms of the center fielder. Harold hit the home run Eddie had been dreaming about.

And just like that, Eddie was happy. He couldn't stop talking about Harold's spectacular home run.

"That ball went so high, it almost hit a bird. And you ran the bases so fast, there was no way they could tag you out, even when they got the ball."

As usual, the kids gathered around Eddie and listened in awe of all the wonderful things they had accomplished. It made them feel like heroes.

But after a while, as Eddie continued, the kids started to drift away.

"That brown-and-white dog that was running up and down near the fence has the funniest-looking tail," he said. "And did you notice the huge mustache on the guy who sells ice cream?"

Eddie looked up and noticed that everyone was gone. He ran to catch up with them.

When Harold saw him, he stopped and motioned to his friends to walk on.

"I'm tired of you tagging along all the time," he told Eddie.

"But I want to play!"

"Why?" Harold demanded. "You're no good at sports. So why do you keep pushing yourself?"

"Because I want to be like you. I want the kids to think I'm great. I want to hear people cheer. And I want you to be proud of me."

Harold put his arm around his brother's shoulder. "Then I have a better idea. Let's try to think of something you do well and really love."

"Well," Eddie answered slowly with a shy smile on his face, "I may not be good at sports, but I like to talk."

"You sure do!" Harold agreed. "Hey, I have an idea." Harold's face lit up with a huge grin. "You could be in the public-speaking contest at the school."

Eddie was excited. "Do you think I could do that?"

Harold knew he had to be honest. "Well, I think you have a chance. But sometimes you don't know when to stop talking. You go on and on. When you talk about the games, you start out telling everyone what they want to hear. But then you get into stuff that they're not interested in. You need to figure out exactly what you want to say, say it, and then stop talking."

"I get it, Harold. I need to stick to the subject. Sometimes I get carried away. I'll try to remember what you've told me," said Eddie.

Every day after school and on weekends, when Harold went out to play ball, Eddie stayed home and worked on his speech.

When Harold came home after playing ball one day, he surprised Eddie by telling him, "The guys asked why you didn't come down to the park. There was no one to give them the wrap-up of the game. They really missed you."

Eddie felt great that the guys had noticed that he wasn't there. "I guess they didn't miss my playing, but they missed my play-by-play. They missed *me*. Harold, do you think I could try out my speech on the team?"

"Sure," Harold replied.

The next day, Eddie met the kids in the park after their game. He stood in front of them and took a folded sheet of paper out of his pocket. "I've been making notes," he said. "Here goes."

When he finished, there was a moment of silence. Then he heard loud applause and cheers from his friends. "Boy, that was great!" someone said.

"You may not be a good ballplayer, but you sure know how to talk," another joined in. Best of all, no one had left before he had finished.

On the big day, Eddie sat on the stage in the school auditorium with all the other kids who had entered the speaking contest. Do I stand a chance? he wondered nervously.

Finally it was his turn. His heart was beating fast and his palms were sweaty. When he saw Harold and his other teammates in the audience, he started to feel better. "The title of my speech is 'Doing What You Do Best,'" he began. And suddenly, as he started talking, he wasn't nervous anymore.

"Can I tell you something? I am a rotten athlete," he said, looking out at the audience. "But I'm finding out that there are other things that I *can* do well. Let me tell you about it." And he did.

When Eddie finished, the whole audience started clapping wildly. Eddie was thrilled, but the best thing of all was seeing Harold there, standing up and cheering for him.

The judges announced the winner of the speaking contest. It was Eddie! They called him to the front of the stage and gave him a big gold medal. On the front it read: For Excellence in Public Speaking.

Harold couldn't have been prouder. "That's my kid brother. Wow! He's a champion talker," he said as the kids gathered around them.

Eddie so loved speaking that from then on he looked for every opportunity to talk in front of an audience.

He grew up and became a lawyer and spoke in front of judges and juries.

Later, he even became the mayor of New York City.

Sometimes Harold would come to hear Eddie speak. Having his brother there made Eddie feel special. "How am I doing?" Eddie would ask him after a speech. And Harold would chuckle and say, "You're doing great!"